Have You Seen a Dinosaur?

Written by
Matthew W. Beres

Illustrations by
Catherine Rose Heller

Have You Seen a Dinosaur?

Written by Matthew W. Beres

Illustrations by Catherine R. Heller

RBB Research and Publishing

Original sing-along song available for download

https://store.cdbaby.com/cd/dinosong

Have You Seen a Dinosaur?

Have you seen the Brontosaurus?

He eats leaves...from trees.

Have you seen the Triceratops?

Where are all my friends, the dinosaurs?

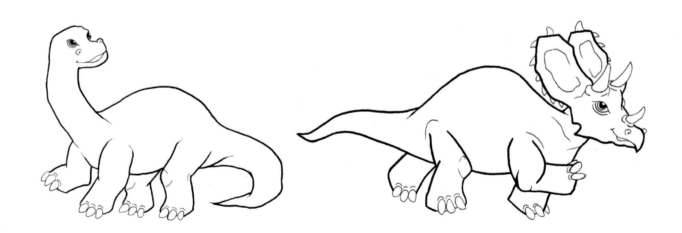

I don't know...nobody knows...

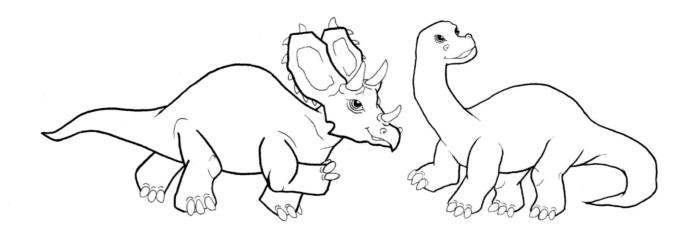

So, if you've seen a dinosaur,
be a friend and let me know.

And now we're going to learn more, about dinosaurs...

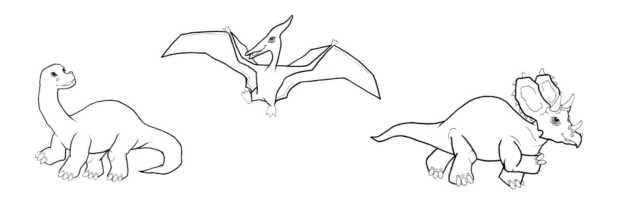

Have you seen the Tyrannosaurus?

She says…

She says...

ROAR!

Have you seen the Pterodactyl?

She has wings...

So she can
SOAR!

Where are all my friends,
the dinosaurs?

Nobody knows...
nobody knows...

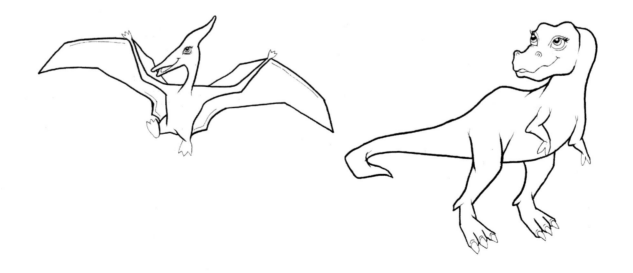

So, if you've seen a dinosaur,
be a friend and let me know.

And now you've learned a bit,
about dinosaurs.

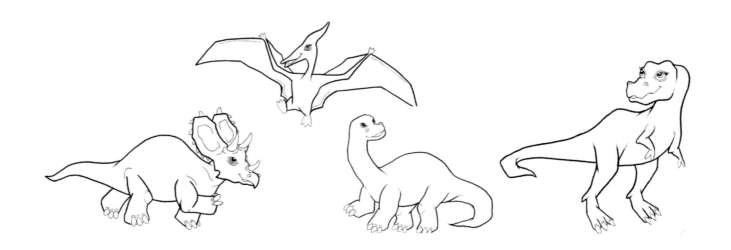

Made in the USA
Columbia, SC
04 January 2020